P9-CQV-547

Ridgefield Library
472 Main Street
Ridgefield, CT 06877
203-438-2282
www.ridgefieldlibrary.org

APR 2 4 2012

Daisy's Perfect Word

Written by Sandra V. Feder

Illustrated by Susan Mitchell

Kids Can Press

To my father, who taught me
how to write, and to my family for
providing the inspiration

— S.V.F.

Contents

Chapter One

On sunny days, Daisy liked picking lemons off the tree in her backyard to make lemonade. She liked playing kickball with her friends and making long dandelion chains, which she wore in her curly hair. On rainy days, Daisy liked putting on her red boots and stomping through puddles, making big, messy splashes.

Almost every day, Daisy rode her bike around the neighborhood with her best friend, Emma. They often stopped to see Mrs. Bookman, who lived on the corner. Mrs. Bookman always had something unusual to eat, like roasted pumpkin seeds, and something interesting to talk about, like how some people are left-handed. "I'm left-dimpled!" Daisy said, smiling to show off the dimple in her left cheek.

But Daisy's favorite part of any day was when she would sit in the shade of the largest tree in her backyard or curl up in her cozy chair with a book in her hands. Daisy liked books because books were full of words.

And more than making lemonade or

wildflower chains or riding her bike with her best friend, Daisy loved words.

She collected her favorite words in a green notebook covered with purple polka dots, and she always took her time deciding which special words should go on each list.

One list was devoted to short words like *fun, great* and *big*. Daisy liked using short words when she was excited, which was a

lot of the time. These words were on a list
in her notebook titled *Wow Words*.

Daisy also liked made-up words.

"*Iska-biska*," she said to Emma as they
walked to school.

"*Ilpa-dilpa*," Emma answered back,
because she liked making up words, too.
Daisy had a whole list of made-up words and
an explanation of what each word meant,
so she wouldn't forget how to use it.

At night when she was sleepy, Daisy liked
quiet words. After saying good-night to her
little sister, Lily, and being tucked in by her
parents, Daisy looked at the list of *Quiet-Time*

Words in her notebook. She whispered *hush-a-bye* and *sweet dreams* to the three teddy bears that slept on her bed.

Usually Daisy fell right asleep. But on nights when she had something important on her mind, she had trouble settling down. This was one of those nights.

Daisy's teacher, Miss Goldner, had told the class that she had some big news to share the next day. Daisy couldn't wait to find out what it was.

Emma and Daisy had wondered about it all the way home.

"I bet we're going to have field trips every week for the rest of the year," Emma said.

"I think we're going to get pizza every day in the cafeteria," Daisy said.

"Maybe the President is going to ask us to help run the country!" Emma exclaimed.

"Maybe the Queen is coming for tea!" Daisy declared.

Now, as Daisy lay in bed, she couldn't help wondering some more. Her teacher had sounded excited, so it must be good news. The ice-cream truck would be permanently parked outside the school? They would be having two hours of reading time every day? Or maybe it was something even bigger. The space program wanted to try sending kids into space, and Daisy's class had been selected? The chocolate maker in town needed some new flavors and wanted students to be tasters?

Daisy finally drifted off to sleep. She dreamed she was in space having tea with the Queen. Instead of little sandwiches, there were chocolate bars with names like MarsMallow Mash and Sweet Saturn Squares. "Delicious," said the Queen, dabbing daintily at her mouth with a napkin. "We must start serving these at the palace."

"Splendid!" Daisy replied, reaching for just one more.

Chapter Two

The next morning, Daisy rushed through her
breakfast, not even taking time to finish her
cinnamon toast. After her crazy dream, she
couldn't wait to get to school to find out her
teacher's big news.

Even though she was in a hurry, Daisy still
tried to avoid walking with Samantha, who
lived next door. Samantha was in Daisy's class
and liked the words *stop* and *mine*.

If they did walk together, Samantha would

always say, *"Slow down,"* and *"Follow me."*
The words Samantha used hurt Daisy's ears.
She didn't want those kinds of words stuck in
her head all day long—not when there were
so many other wonderful words in the world.
When she did walk with Samantha, Daisy
would sometimes hum a little song to herself
when Samantha began to talk.

Avoiding Samantha took some work,
because Samantha was a whole head taller
than Daisy and could easily see over the fence
that separated their houses. Daisy had figured
out that if she cut through her backyard
and then through Mrs. Bookman's bushes,

she could end up in front of Emma's house without ever going by Samantha's house. The only problem was that the bushes were prickly and the ground was muddy, and today she was wearing her new ballet flats and favorite blue hoodie in honor of Miss Goldner's big news.

So Daisy decided to skip, while singing loudly, with her hood pulled up over her head and her eyes closed. Well, one eye really.

She thought it would be a good idea to keep one eye open, so she could see where she was going. Daisy figured Samantha would have no idea what to make of such a spectacle. Besides, Daisy knew that Samantha did not like to skip. By the time Daisy got to the corner, Emma was already there and Samantha hadn't appeared.

All the way to school, Daisy and Emma talked about Miss Goldner—the best teacher in the whole world.

"I like how Miss Goldner uses words like *imagine* and *recess*," Daisy said. "Those words are on my *Sparkling School Words* list."

"After we've been working hard, it's great when Miss Goldner puts her hands on her hips and says, 'You know what we need right now? A dance break!'" Emma said.

"I know!" Daisy agreed. "And she's not like those other teachers who just sit and watch us dance or sort of sway back and forth."

"She's always right in the middle of the class, swinging her arms and twirling around," Emma said. Then Emma, with her long hair bouncing up and down against her back, did an imitation of Miss Goldner's dancing technique right there on the sidewalk.

"She's the best," Daisy agreed, her brown curls flying as she joined in.

"Wasn't it fun when she let us bring our wagons to school covered with white sheets, and we got to travel across the field like pioneers?" Emma asked, resuming the walk to school.

"My favorite day was when we went on that field trip to the beach and our only assignment was to watch the ocean," Daisy said.

"And remember when she made us a cake with different colored layers to teach us about the layers of the earth?" Emma asked.

Daisy remembered it all.

But for Daisy, the absolutely best thing about Miss Goldner was that whenever she used a difficult word, she stopped and explained what it meant. To Daisy, that was the best possible thing a teacher could do.

Daisy was thinking about words and Emma was still enjoying her memory of the cake as they turned the corner and arrived at school.

The girls put their backpacks on the hooks outside the classroom door. Daisy carefully carried her notebook into the classroom and put it inside her desk for safekeeping. When all the children were sitting in their seats,

Miss Goldner did what she always did—she took attendance and said something kind after each student had answered.

"Emma?" she asked.

"Here," Emma said.

"Your shiny headband really makes your eyes sparkle," Miss Goldner said. "And thank you for remembering to water the class plants." Miss Goldner even had something nice to say to Samantha. Daisy usually looked forward to Miss Goldner's comments, but today she could barely sit still. Finally, Miss Goldner put away her attendance folder. Daisy and Emma shot each other looks across

the room. They could hardly wait for the
big announcement.

Miss Goldner stood up tall and asked, "Are
you ready for my big news?" The children all
answered together, "Yes!"

"I'm engaged," Miss Goldner said with a
big smile on her face.

Chapter Three

Daisy loved the sound of *engaged*. It sounded as if it must be splendid. And when Miss Goldner explained what an engagement was—a promise to be married—Daisy knew it was splendid. But it was also sad, because at the end of the school year, Miss Goldner would be moving away.

"I'm very happy," Miss Goldner said, "but I will miss all of you very much." Then her eyes got misty and a couple of tears fell down her cheeks.

That happened every so often, especially when Miss Goldner was talking about a favorite book or something someone had done that was particularly nice. When her tears slipped out, she always apologized to the children saying, "I can't help it. I get very emotional." Not only did Daisy like the word *emotional*, she thought it was part of what made Miss Goldner so special. This time Miss Goldner's emotional moment passed quickly, because the children distracted her with questions.

"What does your wedding dress look like?"
Samantha asked.

"It will be white with little pearls and a skirt
as big and fluffy as a cloud," Miss Goldner said.

"What kind of cake will you have?"
Will asked.

"Chocolate, of course."

"Don't you want to teach at our school anymore?" Ben asked.

"I love this school," Miss Goldner said. "But I will have to move to a new town and find a new school, so I can be with my new husband."

"That sounds like a lot of 'new,'" Emma said.

"It sure does," Miss Goldner agreed, sighing.

Hearing all this, Daisy felt emotional herself and was glad that the recess bell rang before anyone saw the tear in her eye.

Chapter Four

After school, all the children could talk about was Miss Goldner's engagement. Samantha was talking so excitedly that Daisy forgot to hum and listened instead. "I'm going to get Miss Goldner a gift, maybe a vase or candlesticks," Samantha said. For once, Daisy was glad she had listened to Samantha.

Giving Miss Goldner an engagement gift was a good idea, although Daisy thought vases and candlesticks were kind of boring.

The other children wanted to give her gifts, too. Will, who was good at art, said he would make a picture frame. Ben, who loved sports, wondered if Miss Goldner would like a football.

"Let's all bring our presents in on Friday," Samantha said, and the others agreed.

On the way home, Daisy was quiet, while Emma chatted excitedly.

"I wish we could go to the wedding," Emma said. "I bet Miss Goldner will look like a princess! And chocolate cake is my favorite."

It was Daisy's favorite, too. Normally, Daisy would have loved discussing whether the frosting was likely to be buttercream or whipped cream. But today, she was thinking about other, even more important things.

Daisy said good-bye to Emma and headed into her house to tell her mother the big news.

"Miss Goldner is engaged!" Daisy said, dropping her backpack on the floor and climbing onto a stool at the counter. "That word is going on a new list of *Wedding Words*."

"Well, that's wonderful!" Daisy's mother said.

"No … I mean … yes, it is," Daisy responded. "It's great she's getting married, but then she will have to move away. She won't teach at our school anymore. I won't be able to go visit her next year and show her my new word lists," Daisy explained. "And I won't get to see her at lunchtime or recess."

"Oh, I see," said her mother.

Just then, Daisy's little sister, Lily, walked into the kitchen, wearing her purple superhero cape, fastened with a big gold clasp. Lily pushed her bangs out of her eyes and handed Daisy a card she had made at preschool.

"It's for you," Lily said, with her hands on her hips, in her best superhero stance. "For my big sister."

Daisy took the card and looked at it. It had a big flower on the front and her name written in bright orange letters inside. The "D" was printed backwards.  It made Daisy smile, even though she didn't much feel like smiling. Daisy gave Lily a hug.

"I want to get Miss Goldner an engagement present," Daisy said, returning to her seat at the counter.

"How about something for the kitchen?" her mother suggested.

"That's a good idea," Daisy said, "but I want to get something special."

"Something homemade is always nice," her mother said. Daisy looked at the card her sister had given her. It was nice. Daisy was good with clay and made great friendship bracelets, but those didn't seem right either.

"Even more special," Daisy said.

Daisy's mother stopped stirring the sauce she was making for dinner and looked at Daisy. She knew that look of determination.

It was the same look Daisy had when she decided that for her book report project, she would decorate a soda bottle to look like the book's main character.

There was much glue, tape and fabric involved in the project, not to mention Styrofoam, buttons and yarn. It had taken Daisy days of work to make it look just right. But when she was finished and brought her creation to school, Miss Goldner said that it was the most wonderfully creative book report she had ever seen. It was still displayed prominently on a shelf above Miss Goldner's desk.

"I don't think you need any more suggestions from me right now," her mother said. "I can tell you're going to come up with your own idea, and I bet it will be just right."

* * *

That afternoon, her mom made Daisy's favorite snack—a big bowl of strawberries with vanilla yogurt. Between bites, Daisy did what she always did when she had serious thinking to do. She pressed her nose up against the

fishbowl that was home to her goldfish, Bubbles. Bubbles was a special, one-of-a-kind fish that came when Daisy called his name. She had found that staring at Bubbles and the clear water usually helped her see things more clearly. But this time, it didn't help. She slumped over her strawberries.

Daisy wanted to get Miss Goldner a one-of-a-kind present so Miss Goldner would never forget her, even when she moved away and had a whole new group of students to teach. But Daisy didn't know what that present should be.

Daisy thought some more. She got up from the counter and paced around the kitchen.

Still nothing was coming to her. So she grabbed a book and went outside to sit under her favorite tree, a large oak. But instead of reading, she tried to do some more thinking.

She thought about the best gifts she had ever received. There was the pink elephant her grandfather gave her the day she was born, the ball from her uncle that bounced so high it ended up stuck on the roof, and the watch from her aunt that came with a different band for each day of the week. Then there was the special piece of brown sea glass that Emma had given her because it was the same color as Daisy's eyes. They were all wonderful gifts, but none of them seemed quite right for Miss Goldner.

Finally, she gave up thinking for a while. She watered the herbs her mother had planted, jumped rope and picked some lemons from the lemon tree. Still nothing. When she came back in, she put her book away in her backpack and saw her green notebook with the purple polka dots. She picked it up and turned it over in her hands.

Then it came to her.

Daisy would find Miss Goldner the perfect word! A word she would know was chosen specially for her. It would be a word that was right for kids and teachers, perfect loudly or softly, and not too long or too short. Plus, it would be full of fun. She would find a perfect word for a perfect teacher. But what would it be?

Chapter Five

Daisy gobbled down the rest of the strawberries and ran back outside. She yelled, "Yippee!" and did a happy dance on the lawn, her curls bobbing up and down. She was so eager to start her search that she didn't even mind when Samantha leaned over the fence and said, *"Be quiet!"*

All of a sudden the sun peeked out from behind the clouds. *Yellow* was a good word, not too long and not too short. But then again, maybe it was a little too, well, *yellow*. What if Miss Goldner was having a *blue* day? In that case, *yellow* would not work at all.

Daisy opened the front door and told her mom, "I'm going to Emma's house."

She raced down the block.

"I'm going to find the perfect word for Miss Goldner!" Daisy called to Emma, who was in her front yard. "Want to help?"

"Sure," said Emma. "Where do we start?"

Daisy looked around.

"I guess we start right here," Daisy replied.

Daisy was used to looking for things. Almost every morning, Lily seemed to have misplaced one of her shoes, and Daisy could never find a sharpened pencil when she needed it. She had a magnifying glass and detective's hat for when she and Emma wanted to solve mysteries. But even Daisy wasn't exactly sure how to find a perfect word for someone.

"*Rose?*" she said, noticing the lovely flowers in Emma's garden. Daisy pulled the yellow blossom toward her to smell it, but a thorn pricked her finger. "Ouch!" she said. It was not quite perfect.

"*Lawn?*" Emma asked.

"No," Daisy said. "Sounds too much like *yawn.*"

The girls watched what was going on around them.

"*Hummingbird!*" Emma yelled, pointing excitedly. Daisy did love the word hummingbird, because it combined the idea of a bird with the sound the bird makes — humming. Daisy thought that was fantastic! But fantastic as it was, she didn't think it was right for Miss Goldner.

She and Emma needed a change of scenery.

"Let's go for a ride," Daisy said.

"Where to?" Emma asked.

"Sweetums?" Daisy suggested.

"Yep," said Emma. "I'll tell my mom we're going."

* * *

Sweetums was the best candy store in the world. Not because it had the biggest selection, or because it had the most unusual candies.

It was the best because Daisy and Emma could ride their bikes there, and because Sweetums had plenty of candy, displayed in pretty glass jars, that only cost a dime or a quarter.

"Are you going to get a red licorice?" Daisy asked, knowing that was one of Emma's favorites.

Licorice was on Daisy's list of *Sweetest Words* along with *caramel* because both were a little unusual. *Taffy* was also on there, because it was so much fun to say, and *chocolate* was at the top of the list, because it was Daisy's favorite.

"I'm thinking it might be a *peppermint* sort of day," Emma answered.

Daisy wasn't sure which candy to get. She always chose some kind of chocolate. But she was worried that she was getting to be a bit like her cousin, who always examined every flavor of ice cream at the ice-cream store, and even tasted a few, but always ordered the same thing—vanilla. Maybe she should try something that wasn't chocolate. She compromised, settling on a chocolate with butterscotch in the center.

"What did you get for Lily?" Emma asked, because she knew Daisy liked to surprise Lily with little gifts. Daisy had picked out a pink taffy. When the girls got home, Lily was playing out front. She was wearing her pink leotard with the matching tutu, which were recent birthday presents, and which she hardly ever took off.

"Close your eyes," Daisy said, and Lily obliged.

Then Lily put out her hand and tilted her face up. Daisy placed the surprise in Lily's open palm and signaled for her to open her eyes by pushing gently on Lily's little nose. "Taffy!" Lily said. "Yumm!" Daisy thought about the word *taffy* for Miss Goldner. But then she remembered that Miss Goldner preferred chocolates with cream centers.

Before dinner, Daisy went back to Emma's house to do some homework, but she had a hard time concentrating. Maybe Miss Goldner would like a practical school word like *eraser* or *subtraction*. She wrote those words down on a piece of scrap paper, but then she crossed them out. Those words might be useful, but they weren't very exciting. Daisy's mother called to tell her it was time to come home for dinner. "It's spaghetti night," Daisy said to Emma. "I don't want to be late, or Lily might eat all the meatballs."

That night, Daisy told her family about her plan to find the perfect word for Miss Goldner. Lily suggested *blankie*, because everyone feels better with a blankie. Her mother suggested *coffee*, because she said a lot of grown-ups feel better with coffee. Her father suggested *vacation*, because he said most people feel better after taking one. Daisy listened carefully to each idea but knew she hadn't found the right word yet.

Later, as Daisy said her good-nights to her teddy bears, she wondered if Miss Goldner might like a *Quiet-Time* word. After all, everyone needed to go to sleep.

But Daisy decided that her *Quiet-Time* words might be better for kids and stuffed animals than for teachers. She would have to keep looking.

Chapter Six

The next day was science day. Daisy and Emma were eager to get to school, because Miss Goldner always made science fun.

When they walked into the classroom, they were dazzled by what they saw. Miss Goldner had hung two-dozen little crystals on strings from the ceiling. The crystals were creating rainbows all over the room.

"It's beautiful," Emma said.

"It's magical!" Daisy declared.

All the other children "oohed" and "aahed" as they came in. Miss Goldner explained that the crystals were actually prisms. The prisms separated out each color contained in white light, causing the rainbows to appear.

At each child's desk was a little prism to use. Before Daisy picked hers up, she took out her notebook and started a new list: *Rainbow Words*. She wrote down *light* and *colors*. Then she thought for a minute and added *magical*. Hmm. Maybe *rainbow* would be a good word for Miss Goldner. It sure was full of brightness. But it was a little too light and airy. It wasn't quite perfect.

After school, Emma had to go to dance class, and Daisy went to visit Mrs. Bookman. While she was at school, Daisy had decided that a visit with Mrs. Bookman was just what she needed.

"Well, hello, Daisy," Mrs. Bookman said when she opened the door. "Rhubarb pie?"

Daisy wasn't sure what a rhubarb was, but Mrs. Bookman's unusual foods were almost always tasty, and who wouldn't want pie?

"I need to call my mom to let her know I'm here," Daisy said, picking up the phone as Mrs. Bookman put two large slices of pie onto plates.

Rhubarb pie turned out to be sweet and a little tart at the same time. Daisy thought it would go nicely with her homemade lemonade and promised Mrs. Bookman she would bring some over the next time she made a pitcher.

One of the great things about Mrs. Bookman was that she always treated kids as if they were grown-ups, asking their opinions about important things like whether she should paint her living room peach or beige. Daisy thought peach would be peachy.

Mrs. Bookman was also a good listener.
Daisy had been wondering about the word
indigo. "If it's a color in the rainbow, it must
be pretty important," Daisy said. "But no one
ever says, 'I just got indigo sneakers.'"

Mrs. Bookman nodded and said, "I never thought about that, but you're absolutely right!"

Daisy explained what she was looking for today—the perfect word for her teacher.

"Ah, yes," Mrs. Bookman said. "There are many wonderful words—musical ones, theatrical ones and just plain useful ones. But I'm not sure I've ever noticed a perfect one."

Daisy sighed.

"Sometimes the best things are the hardest to find," Mrs. Bookman said. "Listen to the world around you, and I'm quite certain you will be successful."

Daisy did not feel certain at all and wasn't quite sure how to listen to the world. Still, she was glad Mrs. Bookman hadn't said the quest was impossible. Daisy thanked her for the pie and promised to come again soon.

Chapter Seven

On her way back home, Daisy walked by Samantha's house. Just her luck, Samantha was playing hopscotch on the sidewalk.

"I found the perfect vase for Miss Goldner," Samantha said. "A vase is very practical. It's something Miss Goldner can always use."

Daisy imagined Miss Goldner happily arranging flowers in Samantha's vase. She imagined Miss Goldner giving Samantha a big hug. She imagined herself looking at the floor, because she didn't have any gift at all.

When Daisy arrived back home, her mother saw her slumped shoulders. "I know how difficult it can be," her mother said. "Sometimes when I'm writing something, I just can't think of the right word but eventually it comes. Try not to get discouraged." Daisy went to her room and took out the little paperback dictionary she had gotten as a birthday present the previous year. She looked up *discouraged*. When she learned that it meant to feel a lack of hope and spirit, she opened her notebook and added it to her list of *Words for Difficult Times*.

When her dad came home from work, he found Daisy outside, lying on the grass, staring up at the sky. "Want to play some catch?" he asked.

"Sure," she said, grabbing her mitt. They tossed the ball back and forth. "What's your favorite word?"

He thought for a minute.

"I guess I'd have to go with *baseball*," he said.

Baseball was a word that made Daisy think of lots of fun things — hot dogs, sunshine, the smell of her mitt, the feel of the ball in her hand and the wonderful "crack" the bat made when it hit the ball.

"*Baseball* is a great word," she said. "But I'm pretty sure Miss Goldner plays tennis."

Daisy was beginning to doubt whether she would ever find the perfect word for Miss Goldner. And if she did find it, would Miss Goldner be able to use it?

But Daisy didn't want to give up, so she
went inside, got out her notebook and turned
to her list of *Encouraging Words*. She read
from the list: *try, effort* and *smile*. Daisy went
to the mirror and said to her reflection,
"Keep trying," and gave herself a smile
big enough that she could see the dimple
in her left cheek.

Chapter Eight

The next morning Daisy was determined to avoid Samantha, so she risked the shortcut through the prickly bushes and ended up with only a couple of scratches. She wanted to walk just with Emma, because they had so much to talk about.

"I'm so excited you get to spend the night tonight, and it's a school night," Daisy said.

"My parents usually don't have to be out so late, but tonight they have to go to an office party," Emma said. "And my babysitter has to be home earlier. It's great your mom said I could stay with you."

"Cupcakes or brownies?" Daisy asked.

"Brownies," Emma replied.

"Sleeping bags or sheets and blankets?" Daisy wondered.

"Sleeping bags," Emma voted.

"I won't be able to play the whole time," Daisy said, "because I still haven't found the perfect word for Miss Goldner."

"You will," Emma said with such confidence that Daisy was reminded all over again why they were best friends.

At recess and lunch, they continued making plans for their sleepover and were so excited that they leapt out of their seats when the bell rang at the end of the day. Daisy went home to get out the sleeping bags and to start baking the brownies, while Emma headed to her house to pack her overnight bag. Daisy decided to do a little word thinking while she waited. Brownies are yummy, but the word *brownie* made her think more about the color than about how good brownies taste.

Finally, Emma rang the doorbell, and Daisy raced to let her in. After getting Daisy's room all set up, the girls finished their homework. They were in the middle of a great pillow fight when Daisy's mother said, "Stop being so rambunctious." Hmm. *Rambunctious* was one of those words that felt perfect in Daisy's mouth, but she wasn't exactly sure what it meant. She whacked Emma one last time with her pillow.

"Please come set the table," Daisy's mother called. Daisy and Emma laid out the plates, cups and silverware. Lily folded the napkins.

"Dinner smells marvelous," Daisy's father said as he entered the kitchen.

Marvelous, Daisy thought. It was definitely good for saying loudly but not so good for quiet times. It was not quite perfect, even though her mother's macaroni and cheese was quite marvelous.

"How's your word search going?" Daisy's dad asked.

"I've found some great words, but not the perfect one for Miss Goldner," Daisy said.

"Sometimes, when I have a problem I'm trying to solve, I give myself a little time off from thinking about it," her dad said.

"But tomorrow is the day everyone is giving their gifts," Daisy explained.

"I got Miss Goldner a photo album, so she can take pictures of us and show them at her new school," Emma said. Everyone at the table agreed that a photo album was a thoughtful gift. "You can help me wrap it," Emma offered.

Daisy wasn't so sure that taking time off from her quest to find the perfect word for Miss Goldner was a good idea, but she was tired of looking and didn't feel much closer to finding the right word than when she'd begun. Besides, she didn't want to miss out on a minute of the fun she and Emma had planned. "I'll just take a little break," Daisy said.

So after dinner, the girls listened to music and danced around the living room. They made a tunnel out of cushions for Lily to crawl through. They watched a silly show on television and ate brownies. After that, Daisy offered to put Lily to bed, because sometimes just being with Lily made Daisy feel better.

They read Lily's favorite story, about a fairy who has trouble turning a prince back into a frog. Daisy tucked Lily in. "Here comes the tickle monster!" Daisy whispered, holding up her hands and wiggling her fingers. As Daisy tickled her, Lily laughed and laughed. And that's when it came to Daisy—the perfect word for Miss Goldner! Daisy couldn't believe her good luck. She kissed Lily good-night and ran back to her room. The word was so perfect that she wrote it in her notebook on its very own page.

Chapter Nine

The next day at school, Samantha handed
Miss Goldner a big package wrapped in silver
paper. Miss Goldner opened the box and
admired the vase inside. Some of the other
children had brought gifts, too — bubble
bath, a little container in the shape of an
apple, a hand-made picture
frame, a football and
lots of wonderful
homemade

cards with lovely messages written inside.

Miss Goldner thanked all the children and told them how much she would miss them, especially when she needed a dance break. Then her eyes got a little misty and a couple of tears rolled down her cheeks.

Daisy knew it was time. She took a deep breath and raised her hand.

"I got you a present, too," she said. Miss Goldner looked around. "Oh, it's not in a box or an envelope," Daisy said.

Miss Goldner looked surprised.

"I found you the perfect word," Daisy said proudly.

"That's ridiculous," said Samantha. "There's no such thing as a perfect word." Daisy wanted to hum, but she didn't. This moment was too important.

"This word is perfect for Miss Goldner," Daisy said. "It's great for saying loudly and for whispering softly. It's not too long or too short, and I know both kids and grown-ups like it. It's not a made-up word, but it sounds like it could be, and it sure feels good in your mouth."

"Well," said Miss Goldner, wiping her eyes, "I can hardly wait."

Chapter Ten

"What is it?" Miss Goldner asked,

leaning in close to make sure she could hear.

"*Giggle*," Daisy said.

Then she extended both her hands toward

Miss Goldner with a little flourish and said,

"Now, you try."

"*Giggle*," said Miss Goldner, smiling.

"*Giggle*," said Emma, breaking into a grin.

"*Giggle*," said Ben, starting to giggle.

By the time the rest of the students tried it,

the whole class was laughing, even Samantha.

Soon there was such laughter coming from Room 8 that the principal, Mrs. Joseph, came walking briskly down the hall. When she entered the room, all the children tried their best to stop laughing. But it was no use.

"It's my gift," Daisy tried to explain. "The word *giggle*," she managed to get out before she burst into another round of giggles.

Mrs. Joseph wasn't at all sure she understood what was going on in Room 8, but she loved her students to be happy and these children certainly were happy.

In fact, they were so happy they were all laughing—every single one.

So Mrs. Joseph let out a big laugh herself and returned to her office.

Chapter Eleven

That afternoon Daisy and Emma walked home from school with Samantha. They talked about the day at school, and Samantha used words like *great* and *fun*. Daisy didn't hum at all.

Emma left them at the corner to go to her house.

"'Bye, Daisy," Samantha said as she turned to walk up her driveway. "Yours was the best gift of all."

Samantha's words fell like little presents on Daisy's ears.

"Thanks," Daisy said.

As she ran up the lawn to her house, Daisy let out a big *yippee*! And Samantha didn't even say, *"Be quiet."*

In fact, Daisy thought she heard a little *giggle*.

Daisy's Wonderful Word Lists

MADE-UP WORDS

coolio — super

Iska-biska — How are you?

Ilpa-dilpa — Fine, thank you.

Mahatzi — Let's go!

glubby — feeling blah

WOW WORDS

great

big

fun

hop

red

SPARKLING SCHOOL LIST

create

imagine

recess

cooperate

art

learn

QUIET-TIME WORDS

good-night

snuggle

hush-a-bye

lullaby

sweet dreams

SWEETEST WORDS

chocolate!!!!!!

taffy

caramel

licorice

honey

fudge

WEDDING WORDS

engagement

bridesmaid

bouquet

Something old, something new, something borrowed,

something blue

RAINBOW WORDS

colors

indigo

light

magical

WORDS FOR DIFFICULT TIMES

blue

discouraged

down

sad

unhappy

ENCOURAGING WORDS

good

smile

effort

happy

try

try again

Daisy's Golden Glossary

Giggle — to laugh

Emotional — showing strong emotions

Engagement — a promise to be married

Indigo — a color that is between blue and violet
in the rainbow

Prism — a clear object that breaks up light
into all the colors of the rainbow

Rambunctious — active and noisy, hard
to control

Splendid — grand, excellent, very fine

Giggle!

Text © 2012 Sandra V. Feder
Illustrations © 2012 Susan Mitchell

All rights reserved. No part of this publication may be reproduced, stored in a
retrieval system or transmitted, in any form or by any means, without the prior
written permission of Kids Can Press Ltd. or, in case of photocopying or other
reprographic copying, a license from The Canadian Copyright Licensing Agency
(Access Copyright). For an Access Copyright license, visit www.accesscopyright.ca
or call toll free to 1-800-893-5777.

This is a work of fiction and any resemblance of characters to persons living or
dead is purely coincidental.

Kids Can Press acknowledges the financial support of the Government of Ontario,
through the Ontario Media Development Corporation's Ontario Book Initiative;
the Ontario Arts Council; the Canada Council for the Arts; and the Government
of Canada, through the BPIDP, for our publishing activity.

Published in Canada by
Kids Can Press Ltd.
25 Dockside Drive
Toronto, ON M5A 0B5

Published in the U.S. by
Kids Can Press Ltd.
2250 Military Road
Tonawanda, NY 14150

www.kidscanpress.com

Edited by Sheila Barry
Designed by Marie Bartholomew

CM 12 0 9 8 7 6 5 4 3 2 1
Manufactured in Shen Zhen, Guang Dong, P.R China,
in 10/2011 by Printplus Limited

Library and Archives Canada Cataloguing in Publication

Feder, Sandra V., 1963–
     Daisy's perfect word / written by Sandra V. Feder ; illustrations by
Susan Mitchell.

ISBN 978-1-55453-645-0

I. Mitchell, Susan, 1962– II. Title.

PZ7.F334Da 2012.   j813'.6   C2011-904724-1

Kids Can Press is a /@r\S™ Entertainment company